Little Red Riding Hood

For Mirren and Gowan, from a mum who says
please *don't* always stay on the path! — L. D.

To Noemi T. Bergere — C. C.

Barefoot Books
294 Banbury Road
Oxford, OX2 7ED

Barefoot Books
2067 Massachusetts Ave
Cambridge, MA 02140

Text copyright © 2012 by Lari Don
Illustrations copyright © 2012 by Célia Chauffrey
The moral rights of Lari Don and Célia Chauffrey have been asserted
Story CD narrated by Imelda Staunton
Recording and CD production by Sans Walk Spoken Word Studio, England

First published in Great Britain by Barefoot Books, Ltd
and in the United States of America by Barefoot Books, Inc in 2012
The hardback edition with story CD first published in 2012
The paperback edition with story CD first published in 2012

Graphic design by Penny Lamprell, Lymington
Reproduction by B & P International, Hong Kong
Printed in China on 100% acid-free paper
This book was typeset in Dutch Mediaeval Pro and Liam
The illustrations were painted in extra-fine Liquitex acrylic,
with small details picked out in artist's pencils

Hardback ISBN 978-1-84686-766-8
Paperback ISBN 978-1-84686-768-2

British Cataloguing-in-Publication Data:
a catalogue record for this book is available from the British Library

Library of Congress Cataloging-in-Publication Data is
available under LCCN 2012009603

1 3 5 7 9 8 6 4 2

562 1447

Little Red Riding Hood

Barefoot Books

Step inside a story

Once upon a time, a little girl wanted to visit her granny in the forest.

She wrapped herself in the new red cloak Granny had sewn for her, then picked up her basket.

"Carry that carefully, Little Red Riding Hood," said her mother. "It's full of cakes and bottles of lemonade. Don't stop to play in the woods. And don't eat the cakes. Just go straight to Granny's cottage!"

Little Red Riding Hood walked into the forest, deep in the shadow of the trees. She felt like the only person there. She clutched the basket, and walked in the middle of the path.

Then she heard a voice. "Hello, little girl!"

She smiled. She wasn't alone at all!

She turned round and saw a handsome wolf leaning against a tree.

The wolf smiled, showing his long white teeth.
"Where are you off to, my dear?" he asked.

"I'm taking cakes to my granny. Would you like a bite?"
She showed him the cakes in the basket.

"No, thank you. I don't eat cake." He smiled again.
"Do you have far to go? Where is your granny's house?"

"She lives in the middle of the forest, in a clearing with a
river running behind the cottage. And she has roses, and a rock
garden, and apple trees, and she never bothers to lock her . . ."
Little Red Riding Hood stopped. She shouldn't tell secrets
to a stranger.

The wolf peered into the basket. "Oh, dear! You're only taking cakes and lemonade. Once she's finished those, she'll have nothing to remind her of your visit. Could you take something else, something which will last a few days?" He frowned and looked around.

Little Red Riding Hood looked around. "I could take flowers!" she said.

"What a clever girl! You can pick flowers on the way. Now, I have to go and prepare my lunch, so farewell, and be careful in the forest."

Little Red Riding Hood waved at the wolf as he loped
off through the trees. Then she walked slowly along the
winding path, picking a big bunch of flowers.

The wolf ran through the forest towards the small cottage.
He didn't stop to pick any flowers at all, so he got to Granny's
cottage before Little Red Riding Hood.

The wolf knocked at the door. A creaky voice called, "Who's that?"

"It's your sweet little granddaughter," sang the wolf in a high voice. "I've brought you some cakes. Can I come in?"

"Come in, come in my dear! The door's open as usual."

The wolf opened the door very quietly and stepped inside.

The wolf bounded up to the bed, opened his mouth WIDE and swallowed Granny in one big gulp.

She vanished, right into his belly, slippers and glasses and all!

The wolf burped and rubbed his belly. Then he wriggled into Granny's spare nightie and spare nightcap and snuggled down into bed.

Little Red Riding Hood stepped through the open door. "Hello, Granny!"

She put the flowers in a vase, put the cakes on a plate, then opened the curtains. When she saw Granny in the sunlight, she said,

"Granny! What big hands you have!"

"All the better to hug you with," the wolf whispered.

She opened the window. When she saw a breeze ruffle Granny's hairy ears, she said,

"Granny! What big ears you have!"

"All the better to hear you with!" the wolf smiled.

She lit the fire. When she saw Granny's face in the firelight, she said,

"Granny! What big eyes you have!"

"All the better to see you with!" the wolf chuckled.

Little Red Riding Hood carried the cakes over to the bed.
When Granny grinned, she said,

"Granny! What big teeth you have!"

"All the better to . . . EAT YOU WITH!"

The wolf opened his mouth WIDE and swallowed
Little Red Riding Hood in one big gulp.

She vanished, right into his belly, cloak and pigtails
and all!

The wolf burped, rubbed his belly and lay
back down.

The wolf was full of Granny and full of little girl, and the bed was warm and soft. Soon he began to snore.

The hunter tracking animals in the forest heard the snores. "That sounds like a wolf!" he thought. He followed the sound to Granny's cottage, looked through the window and saw the wolf with his bulging belly, snoring on the bed.

"I wonder what that wolf has eaten today?" thought the hunter. "His belly looks enormous!"

The hunter tiptoed into the cottage and used his knife to cut the wolf's belly wide open.

saved Granny and Red Riding hood life.

Out came Little Red Riding Hood, coughing and spluttering.

Out came Granny, sneezing and sniffling.

The wolf was still snoring.

Little Red Riding Hood thanked the hunter.
"Let's make sure that wolf never eats anyone else."

She ran out to the garden and dug up seven heavy
stones which she pushed into the wolf's empty belly.
She stitched the wolf up with some thread she found in
Granny's work basket. Then the hunter, Little Red Riding
Hood and Granny hid behind the curtains.

The wolf woke up. He stretched, and burped, and scratched. Then he grabbed a bottle of lemonade and gulped it down.

"I'm still thirsty. That granny must have been too salty." He grabbed the other bottle, and gulped it down.

"I'm STILL thirsty. That little girl must have been too sweet."

So the wolf went outside to get a drink from the river.
When he bent down, the stones in his belly tipped him right
into the water, and he was too heavy to get back out.

That was the end of the wolf.

The hunter returned to the forest with a pocketful of cakes.

Granny locked her door when she went to bed. And Little Red Riding

Hood never turned round to talk to strangers again.

Barefoot Books
step inside a story

At Barefoot Books, we celebrate art and story that opens the hearts
and minds of children from all walks of life, focusing on themes that
encourage independence of spirit, enthusiasm for learning and respect
for the world's diversity. The welfare of our children is dependent on
the welfare of the planet, so we source paper from sustainably managed
forests and constantly strive to reduce our environmental impact.
Playful, beautiful and created to last a lifetime, our products combine
the best of the present with the best of the past to educate our
children as the caretakers of tomorrow.

www.barefootbooks.com

Lari Don was born in Chile and brought up in Scotland. She has worked in politics and for the BBC, but now spends her time collecting and telling stories and making up new ones. She is an award-winning children's author as well as a traditional storyteller, whose love of myths, legends and fables inspires her fiction. Lari lives in Edinburgh with her family.

www.laridon.co.uk

Célia Chauffrey studied graphic design in Paris and illustration in Lyon, and has now illustrated many books with characters and compositions that are always unexpected, fascinating and emotive. She paints in her home in Lyon, France, in a little workshop under the roof which is full of picture books.

www.celia-celiachau.blogspot.com

Imelda Staunton has acted with both the Royal Shakespeare Company and the National Theatre, winning two Olivier awards. Her many screen roles include the title role in *Vera Drake*, which won her a BAFTA and an Academy Award nomination, and Professor Umbridge in two Harry Potter films.